It All Starts in *Paris*

DURSTOLA

The EC Publishing LLC books may be ordered
through booksellers or by contacting:

EC Publishing LLC
116 South Magnolia Ave.
Suite 3, Unit F
Ocala, FL 34471, USA
Direct Line: +1 (352) 644-6538
Fax: +1 (800) 483-1813
http://www.ecpublishingllc.com/

Ordering Information:
Quantity sales. Special discounts are available on quantity purchases by corporations, associations, and others. For details, contact the publisher at the address above.

Printed in the United States of America

Table of Contents

Acknowledgments

SO THANKFUL TO ERIC HINMAN, OUTSTANDING ART WORK FOR THE COVER OF MY BOOK,

I LIKE TO THANK PETER LAZAR MY FRIEND, ALWAYS THERE TO HELP WITH HIS COMPUTER KNOWLEDGE.

I AM SO GRATEFUL FOR MY LONG TIME FRIEND MICHELLE TRAYLOR SHE IS THE ONE WHO MOTIVATED ME, TO WRITE A DIFFERENT VERSION OF MY PREVIOUS BOOK "BLOODY BAR KOCHBA" WHO WAS TOO GRAPHIC FOR HER SENSITIVE NATURE. MICHELLE TRAYLOR IS THE PRESIDENT OF C.O.G LIBRARY. I VALUE TREMENDOUSLY HER METICULOUS READING OF EVERY PAGE. SHE TOOK MUCH OF HER PRECIOUS TIME TO REVIEW, "IT ALL STARTS IN PARIS".

ALL MY DEEPEST THANKS TO MY PRECIOUS DAUGHTER NOUCHKA, IN THE MIDDLE OF HER BATTLE AGAINST CANCER, SHE OFFERED TO EDIT MY BOOK, SHE ALWAYS ENCOURAGES ME IN EVERYTHING I DO.

Dedication

I DEDICATED "IT ALL STARTS IN PARIS" TO OUR CHILDREN AND GRANDCHILDREN. FOR THEM TO LEARN ABOUT IMPORTANT, ACCURATE RELIGIOUS AND HISTORICAL FACTS. WRITTING AS AN EXCITING FICTIONAL TALE SO THEY WILL NOT BE BORED.

Chapter 1

IT ALL STARTS IN PARIS

Standing at Paris' train station's main entrance, under the big clock, Judith Belford held a picture of David Weis. The picture had been taken at an athletic event. David's parents gave it to her while visiting Paris before they left to Israel to start a new life.

She nervously awaited the arrival of David. She wore a white silk dress with matching accessories. David's mother told her that David was 5'10, black short curly hair with piercing blue eyes.

Judith glanced at the clock with six more minutes to wait. She imagined a young man who was constantly running and jumping, kicking, shooting and only interested in winning competitions. David's mother, Sarai, had told her that David was a "very good boy," and surpassed all the best of all the students in his college in Moscow. But, of course, in the eyes of a mother, her children are always the best.

Finally David appeared, scanning the crowd for a person who matched the description he had been given. His eyes alit on a petite, white, silhouette.

The breeze of the summer morning making her dress dance. The large satin green belt around her waist made her look like a Lily of the Valley. As if drawn together by a magnet, they started walking towards each other.

Judith, who was very expressive, graciously extended her hands; exclaiming: "Welcome to Paris! How was your trip?"

Her voice was a melody to David's ears. The moment he took her hands he felt paralysed. It was like a small electric shock went through his body. His mouth opened but nothing came out, his eyes wide open.

That had never happened to him before. Judith tried to retrieve her hands back without success. She was puzzled. (What is wrong with him? Is he mentally off?) Trying to break the tension she asked; "Do you speak French?"

David snapped out of it, as if returning to earth and quickly let go of her hands. In a deep, warm voice he said; "Yes I speak French.. Please Judith excuse my manners. I did not expect you to be so beautiful.....your beauty struck me speechless."

Judith, with brown eyes smiling under her white, veiled hat, her lovely oval face blushing, and her pink plump lips lost all words for a short time. The tone of David's voice was so warm and charming that it enveloped her in a cloud of velvet.

As they turned to leave, a man walked up to David and spoke quietly in Russian. He handed David a bank book along with money, and his phone number letting David know to call him if he needed to get in touch with his friend Gregory. Then made his exit and disappeared into the crowd.

Judith introduced David to the driver of her mother's sedan. David stared around the train station, noticing the architectural differences from Moscow.

Judith said, "My parents are so happy that you are finally here and they are hoping you will stay with us for a while. The three of us are very fond of your parents."

The limo arrived in one the finest neighbourhoods of Paris. Judith parents, Jacques and Lydia, came out to receive David like family with open arms, and so much love and attention. David felt welcomed and never imagined that people so gracious existed!

Chapter 2

VISITING MONTMARTRE

Judith was enthusiastic to introduce Paris to David. She introduced David to many places including Le Louvre, Les Escaliers De La Butte and Le Sacre Coeur, Notre Dame De Paris.

David had a hard time transitioning to this freedom after all he had been through. He always felt the need to watch his back. Since his brother, Ezra, and Judith's sister, Miriam, had been taken from them, he couldn't help but be on guard. When they would go to a restaurant or other public place, he always made sure to sit with his back to the wall in order to observe the entire room and entrance.

Early one afternoon, they visited Montmartre and admired the works of all the street artists. Judith encouraged David to have his portrait sketched.

David exclaimed; "Not unless you sit with me and have the artist sketch both of us!"

The French artist, made funny comments and had them both laughing, telling them, that he would immortalise them in fifteen minutes using charcoal.

Next day, David came down to dinner. Jacques, Judith father, met David at the door to the dining room and said; "Now you will start to learn about Jewish traditions. It will be our privilege to instruct you."

Jacques placed a yarmulke on his head and pinned the blue velvet yarmulke on David's head. It was the first Friday since he had arrived.

Upon entering the dining room, David noticed that Lydia and Judith also had head coverings. The table was laid with their best china, white linens, beautiful flowers, special wine and twisted loaves of bread. Judith's mother, Lydia, lit the menorah and said the Sabbath blessing. Jacques blessed each person at the table before they ate the meal.

The next morning, Jacques invited David to accompany them to the synagogue. David was a Jew but in Moscow they were forbidden to practice their religion, so he never saw his parents praying. Yet he was curious to know more about all those things. David was surprised that the Rabbi conducted the service in French, as he had expected the service to be spoken in Hebrew. He was happy that he could understand, and enjoyed watching the pageantry as the Torah scrolls were carried around the room for the worshipers to touch and kiss.

During the walk home, Jacques told David that before the war, a person had to get to the synagogue early to get a seat. Now, there were plenty of seats empty as so many had died in the concentration camps.

Chapter 3

MEZUZAH

David noticed that every time Judith and her parents entered or exited their house, they touch a small piece of wood on their doorpost. Finally, David said to Judith, " It is strange to me, to see you and your parents so superstitious, to touch a piece of wood and kiss your hand every time you come in or out of your house. In Russia, people touch a piece of wood furniture and say, "I touch wood! All is well."

Judith was dumb founded, she started to laugh hard.

David surprised by her reaction said, "Did I say something funny?"

Judith tried to stop laughing, "Yes it's hilarious! We are not superstitious, we are religious! We touch the Mezuzah as a constant reminder of God's presence with us. It is the mark of God's love. Inside the small wooden case is a tiny parchment on which is inscribed fifteen verses from the book of Deuteronomy, *Hear O Israel, the Lord our God is One* and continues with the command; *Love God with all thy heart, with all thy soul* and ends with a reminder that God's laws must be instilled in our children at home and away from home."

Judith picked up a book on the shelf and kissed it before she opened it, and said, "The Torah is the most revered sacred object of Jewish ritual. It is God speaking to us." Judith read

Deuteronomy chapter 6.. *"And these words which I command you today shall be in your heart. You shall write them on the doorposts of your house and your gates."* Judith close the book and kissed it before putting it back on the shelf.

David was confused, "Judith I truly apologise for my ignorance. What you just taught me today is beautiful and I will start to do as you do."

Chapter 4

LA SORBONNE UNIVERSITY

Judith took David to the Sorbonne University where she attended classes. David was given a battery of tests in order to place him. They were both delighted when he was accepted at the Sorbonne.

The next Saturday morning, David met Judith in the hallway, stopping on the stairs he asks; "Where are you going so finely dressed up this morning?"

Judith smiled and replied; "I am going to an Orthodox synagogue service."

David eagerly jumped the last 3 stairs; "Can I go with you!?"

Judith seemed surprised; "I don't think so...I don't think you will like it. It's so different than my parent's synagogue. It's more a reflection of the original Jewish worship."

David insisted; "But I would like to come with you. I want to learn more about my Jewish roots."

Judith was happy; "Good! But you cannot sit with me. In an Orthodox service men sit with men and the women sit separately, you will also have to wear your yarmulke, and a shawl with Tzit-tzit."

David said; "what are you talking about... shawl ? Tzit-tzit?... Yarmulke I know now since your father put one on my head."

Judith replies; "The shawl you wear on your shoulders. When the Torah is read, you will place it on your head, just follow what the other men do. Tzit-tzit are the fringes on the shawl, meaning different things.

There will be extra shawls at the synagogue. If you are going to come with me you better hurry and put on your jacket or we will be late."

Following the service, everybody gathered together, The men made preparations for a love offering feast that everyone would enjoy. A big long table appeared with a white table cloth. Seemingly out of nowhere, kosher food, smoked fish, bread, cake, and wine were placed on the table. Everyone remained silenced while performing the hand washing ritual. As wine was poured in each glass set on the table including a little bit for each child and plenty for each adult. The Rabbi covered his head with his shawl and poured wine in his cup while reciting, Psalm 23; "My cup runneth over" (as he let the wine run over the brim of the cup.) "Adonai-Elohim, who created the fruit of the vine, be blessed and bless us."

Everyone said; "Amen" and then each one drank including giving a drop to their children.

The room erupted into a cacophony of voices and laughter. The Rabbi and six other men were holding onto each other's shoulders and singing and dancing. Then the children, boys with boys, and girls with girls, gathered in circles to dance and sing.

Judith said to David; "We are singing and dancing and praising God for the great miracle of our salvation from Egypt and for those who came out of the Holocaust alive."

David was impressed with the cantor's deep voice. David whispered; "Judith I really prefer the Orthodox service, the people are so warm and lively."

Two men came up to David and invited him to prayer service the next morning, at 7am. They explained that ten men minimum were required for the daily service, they needed one more man, for the Quorum.

David asked; "Can you explained, why is a Quorum of ten men needed for prayers?"

Rachmiel replied; "The number ten apparently held a particular fascination for the Jews of antiquity. The commandments were ten, Pharaoh was visited with ten plagues, the High Holy Days include ten Days of Penitence, ten generations are recorded between Adam and Noah and between Noah and Abraham. Abraham underwent ten tests of his faith, and so on. God's presence, rests upon any ten who gather in HIS name. This quorum is known as "minyan." This did not mean that private devotions are not acceptable."

David replies; "honestly, I have never attended an Orthodox service before and I don't not know how I could help.

Rachmiel put his hand on David's shoulder and said; "Don't worry, there is always a first time for everything."

David agreed to join them the next morning.

On the walk back home Judith says to David; "Tomorrow you will need to wear a prayer shawl and T'fillin."

David a question mark on his face; "T'fillin? What is a T'fillin?"

Judith, "T'fillin, or phylacteries, are two small boxes that have leather straps attached. Inside the boxes are four separate pieces of parchment that have verses inscribed on them from the books of Exodus and Deuteronomy. They proclaim God's unity, his care for us, and Israel's deliverance from bondage. VOILA!"

David perplexed; "What am I supposed to do with that?"

Judith continues; "The phylacteries are worn in a certain way. Someone will show you how to correctly tie one around your left arm and the other will be tied onto your forehead." Judith was interrupted by an outburst of laughter from David. He was imagining himself in this disguise.

David laughed; "Why do they do these ridiculous things? I am not going to be able to do that and stay serious."

Judith giggled; "Yes, I suppose, but think about that. The way the T'fillin is placed on your arm and forehead help remove from your mind any thoughts of the world and helps you to concentrate on God. Only the men meet each morning for prayer. Don't worry if you can't go each morning. Men attend when they can."

Some weeks later, after frequently attending the Orthodox Synagogue services with Judith, they became friends with a little group of young people in their 20's, most of them attending the same University.

Judith was now 18 and David's 20th birthday just around the corner. The Rabbi and all of their friends surrounded David.

The Rabbi said to David; "It is now time for you to have your Bar Mitzvah since you did not have one when you were thirteen."

David eagerly agreed and was propelled to the center of the service. The Torah was brought to the reading podium and opened. The Rabbi had David repeat a blessing in Hebrew and had him recite the customary Bar Mitzvah prayer, then he kissed the Torah and it was rolled and tied. The Rabbi placed the Torah scroll on David's shoulder and he carried it all around the room with every man following him and chanting the lesson from the Prophets called the Haftarah.

Chapter 5

THAT STRANGE RUSSIAN MAN

The next year and a half, were a whirlwind of activity for both David and Judith. They were absorbed with their studies. Judith majored in political science and minored in foreign languages. David majored in archeology and minored in social sciences.

Several evenings during the week, David attended a Yeshiva to learn Hebrew language. As time progressed, David and Judith became best friends and were inseparable.

One day, soon after finishing their second year at the Sorbonne, Judith and David were walking down their home street in Paris's most exclusive neighbourhood. Every house had the same twelve- foot high double solid wooden gates for vehicles and a solid wood side door for people. Unless the gates or door were opened, it was impossible to see the house behind the wall.

David and Judith entered through the pedestrian door in front of her parent's house. Noticing that her parent's automobile was not there, they went to the private park in the back of the house. They stopped at the pond, where they sat on a bench.

Judith asked David; "For a long time I wanted to ask you, about "that strange Russian man" at the train station when we first meet two years ago."

David took a big breath and said; "The man is a member of a Russian criminal gang whose leader is my friend, Gregori Mikhalov. Gregori was the person who found the two KGB who murdered your sister Miriam and my brother Ezra for defecting to France. Gregori helped me to avenge their deaths. He got my father and mother in a safe place and out of Russia. In exchange, I stayed to teach his men to fight better. I helped Gregori's gang against a rival gang, who was trying to massacre my friend Gregori, including executing the rival gang's leader."

Judith looked at David in shock! and said, "Wow! How many men did you kill ?"

David answered her; "Seven gang members and the two KGB who assassinated Ezra and Miriam, the two KGB who beat up my father and mother and destroyed our home."

Judith nervously laughed and said; "I think, for my own protection, I will have to marry you."

David now 21, never was in love before, but when he saw Judith for the first time at the train station, he was smitten! David's personality was very outgoing, but with his feelings, he was timid and did not know how to express his love for her. Now that he was sure Judith was in love with him, he stood up.

David said; "Is it the Jewish way, or the French way, that a woman should propose?"

Embarrassed, Judith's face became red and confused as she thought, maybe David isn't ready to get married yet, maybe he has someone else in his mind. She swallowed hard.

David Quickly walked around looking for something. He reached up and grabbed a thin flexible jasmine branch from a bush. With his back to Judith, he fashioned a little ring. He turned back to Judith who for once, was quiet. David knelt at her feet and slipped the ring onto her finger.

And said: "Judith Belford, will you marry me?"

She nodded her head in acceptance with tears of joy in her eyes. Their mouths found one another and sealed the agreement with a long deep kiss. Their magic was broken, by the sound of footsteps on the gravel approaching them.

Judith's mother, Lydia, did not look surprised at what she caught sight of. A huge smile on her face showed approval; "Finally, we have something to celebrate! Father is going to be so very happy!"

Chapter 6

ANCESTORS

David and Judith, cherished the times they spent with one another, walking in Paris, and planning their wedding which was to take place soon after they graduated. Some of the plans they made during these outings included someday moving to Israel to live near David's parents. It was during one of these special moments they visited the Bastille. This prison had been the home to both royalty and commoner. They paused to read one of the plaques under a painting of Voltaire.

Judith read the plaque aloud to David; "Francois-Marie Arouet (1694–1778), better known by his pen name, Voltaire. A writer, essayist and philosopher known for his defence of civil liberties including freedom of religion and free trade. He was imprisoned in la Bastille twice during his youth. He was an outspoken supporter of social reform and actively criticised the catholic church dogma." Look David, this is fascinating! Religion has always been a foundation for conflict between people! As a matter of fact, did you know that I am a direct descendant of one of Israel's best known religious leaders,

Rabbi Akiva ben Yosef ? He tried to liberate Judea from the Romans in 132 A D. Not many people know how prominent a part e played in Jewish history."

David curious; "Really? It must feel wonderful to know who your ancestors are. In Russia, they discourage any Jew to do anything, unless you are a scientist, so they can exploit you. I did not even get to know my grandparents, they died in concentration camp in Siberia. The only family I have ever known are my parents and Ezra. Come on! Let's leave this place and go for a walk along the Seine."

As they were walking toward the river, Judith suddenly stopped and exclaimed; "David! This is where my favorite teacher lives, Professor Benjamin Cohen, from Yeshiva school! He is also a Jewish historian and a writer of both history books and political accounts. I haven't seen him for a long time. He was the person who told me of my ancestors. Do you mind if we stop and say hello?"

"Not at all, I'd like to meet him" David answers.

Judith lifts the door knocker. A frail, old lady answers the door.

"Hello! I am ..." Judith begins.

The lady interrupts; "I would know that smile anywhere, dearest Judith! Please, come in with your friend."

Judith introduces Mrs.Cohen to David, and asks; "How is professor Cohen? Is he home?"

Mrs. Cohen replies sadly; "He died four months ago from pneumonia. But I feel his presence everywhere in this house."

Tears filled Judith's eyes as she hugged Mrs. Cohen. She said; "I am so sorry for your loss. I loved and respected him very much."

Mrs. Cohen stood up; "Wait stay here while I get something." Mrs. Cohen returns holding a book and places the book in Judith's hands. It was richly bound in burgundy leather and had the title imprinted in gold. It read, "The Second Jewish Revolt" by Dr. Benjamin Cohen.

Mrs.Cohen spoke; " Right before my husband's death, this book was published. He wanted you to have one of the first copies. It is about your ancestor, Rabbi Akiva." Judith reverently held the book and opened it. She gasped when she saw Professor Cohen's handwriting followed by his signature.

"This book is dedicated to my smartest and favorite student, Judith Bedford. Her passion for history inspired me to further research the facts about her ancestor, Rabbi Akiva Ben Yosef. During my research I discovered that I was a descendant of Eleazar the Rabi (Cohen) who was the uncle of Bar Kochba the second revolution's General."

Judith closed the book and with tears running down her cheeks, said,"I am very honoured, I shall cherish this book forever."

After sharing a cup of tea and cookies, David stood up looking reverently at Mrs. Cohen; "What a delight to have met you! Judith has accepted my proposal and we will be married as soon as we graduate from university. It would please both of us if you can attend the wedding."

Mrs. Cohen's face lit up: "God willing, I would very much like to come."

Chapter 7

YOU HAVE MAIL!

Several weeks later, as David returned home from class, Lydia met him at the door, waving an envelope in the air; "You have mail from Israel!"

David looked forward to his mother's weekly letters. They were always full of fascinating information about Israel and his parent's adventures. He eagerly went to his room to read the latest.

My dearest son, I am so excited about your upcoming wedding. Father and I can hardly wait to come to Paris to be with you and the Belford family. Did I tell you, my newest friend Tamar, plays violin in the orchestra I am a member of.? We have many things in common. I went with Tamar to rare antique coin exhibition. Egyptian, Greek, Roman, and Judaea coins. Tamar was pointing at a big poster that said an auction would be held next week. Next to her was a large display of first and second century coins of Israel. I was fascinated with few coin, the inscription said that it was a Bar Kochba silver shekel circa 133 A.D, the time of the second Jewish revolt. All of a sudden I remembered a story that my mother's father had told me when I was a little girl. It was about a great national hero, Bar Kochba who was my ancestor! He is also your ancestor! Can you imagine? I was rushed home to tell your father, about my new discovery, and you know what? He wasn't surprised at all! It must be because he's a scientist.

The letter went on, but David's mind was enthralled with the information he had just read. That evening, after the blessing at the dinner table.

Lydia asked him; "How are your parents? Is everything well?"

David very excited; "Yes! they send you their love and that they can hardly wait to come for our wedding. There is a particular part you might find interesting." David shared the part about his ancestor story reading out loud for everyone to hear.

Judith threw up her hands and shouted; "I can't believe it! This is ironic for me to be a descendant of Rabbi Akiva and for you to be a descendant of Rabbi Akiva's partner, Bar Kochba, who directed the war for Judea's freedom from the Romans!"

Jacques exclaimed; "We have to celebrate! This is an incredible event! I will go get a bottle of our best champagne!"

The following Sunday, David and Judith, decided to have a picnic. The day was beautiful and they ventured to the Bois De Vincennes. David transported the basket, and Judith carried her precious book. They ate quickly, in anticipation of getting to the book.

Chapter 8

THE SECOND JEWISH REVOLT

After eating, Judith relaxed against a tree and David lay back on the blanket with his hands interlaced behind his head.

Judith started reading aloud the precious book of professor Cohen, about their ancestors. "The Second Jewish Revolt". From time to time, Judith looked at David's face. It was like he was possessed by the story.

David said, "I can sense my ancestor's blood strongly in my veins. I understand his zealousness. All the feelings of hatred and vengeance I have experienced were a result of watching my parent's beatings and the loss of my brother."

Judith continued to read, about the battle of Bettar as David closed his eyes. A strange sensation invaded his mind, he felt like he was his ancestor Bar Kochba. His mind flew into the story, he saw himself in Bar Kochba's body but with more knowledge and advanced strategies like superman with extraordinary effect flying over the enemy, exterminating the whole army by surprise. His imagination was doing things only the imagination can do. He was enjoying himself so much with his imaginative character that he started laughing.....

Judith stopped her reading and asked him, " What? what? Why are you laughing? This is not funny, I don't understand."

David coming back to earth, asked in a serious tone of voice, "You just read about this Rabbi Bar Yorhai's developing Kabbalah, who was reserved only for the very religious chosen Rabbis, it was a Mystical fascination, they regarded as a direct and magical communion with God. Each word and letter of the Sacred Scripture was carefully weighed, had special meaning. The Hebrew letters of the alphabet have numerical equivalents: the letter "Beth," for example, equals two; the name "Dan" equals fifty-four. Out of these bizarre calculations, the Kabbalists figured out the time of Messiah's approach. They decided Bar Kochba was their Messiah..... Hum.. That is very interesting..... Judith do you know what is Kabbalah?

Judith replies; "It is a very advanced meditation to reach a high level of spirituality. I have personally never experienced it, because it is dangerous if you are not with an experienced Rabbi to guide you.

"David intrigued; "I am very curious to know more."

Judith reply; "I must introduce you to a group of student friends at the University, they call themselves Christian, and they state when they pray they receive the Holy Spirit of God who was promised by their leader Jesus Christ, for all those who obey him. They said it is an exquisite feeling, physically they experience a tickling in their spine and a warm flush inside, and a feeling of peace that surpasses all understanding."

David jumping on his feet screaming; "I know! I know what you are describing, I felt it the first time I touched your hand!"

Judith laughing; "That was a different experience, that is called chemistry."

David grabs Judith in his arms and kisses her allover her face. Making her laugh, as they roll in the green grass, holding each other tight.

Judith continues; "My best friend Elisabeth, is the most amazing student in the world..... What a mind! She is a scientist. She studies with passion about history and all the religions. She can teach about Judaism, Islam, Buddhism, Hinduism as well as Christianity. If you want to know anything you need to ask her. When she explains the origin and tradition of any one religion, you will think that she belongs to that religion she is speaking of. She is so passionate, but you know what? She's an Atheist.. why? Because she suffered terribly to see her family tortured and killed before her eyes during the war in Romania.

One day, I will never forget that day.....we went to a party with a couple of Jewish friends. Suddenly a group of Christians called us "Christ Killers!". . Our tiny little Elisabeth, faced all of them and shouted; "You're ignorant!!! If it were not for us Jews, you would never have Jesus Christ! Jesus is the King of the Jews! And all his disciples were Jews! Go and learn about the origin of your religion, then you will come and kiss our feet!"

David exploded with laughter; "I would love to meet Elisabeth, I can surely learn from her."

Judith reply; "Unfortunately you must wait until we go to Israel. She is married to a military man, and she is a scientist working for the government......

Look at that, almost 4 hours since we started to read the book. There's only just a few more pages, let me finish to read."

David released her from his arms.

Judith read; "Ruth saw her husband Bar Kochba retreating toward Bethar and watched in silent terror as five Romans surrounded him.

The Great Bar Kochba had fallen. Rabbi Akiva had been captured and tortured. It was reported his last words were;

"All my life I've been wanting to fulfil the concept of "Love Your God With All Your Heart, With All Your Soul and With All Your Resources"; and now I finally have the chance to obey with joy."

After Judith finished reading, they both sat for a while and thought about the story.

David sadly said; "John Perez was right when he stood up and shouted: "We will not support Bar Kochba in this war!", because as long as you mistakenly claim him to be the messiah, God will not stand behind this war."

Judith replied; "The Romans tried to exterminate all the Jews, but they failed. Hitler's goal was to do the same. He killed close to six million in the Holocaust but he did not achieve his goal, thanks to the Americans.

Chapter 9

THE WEDDING

What a glorious day, thought David, as he looked out over the courtyard from his balcony. It was a warm Spring morning with a light breeze in the air. The rain from the night before made the droplets on the flowers shine like diamonds. David's heart was full of joy to have his parents coming from Israel for this important day. Looking to the sky his thoughts reached out to Ezra his beloved brother.

David whispered; "I miss your presence so much, specially on this very important step in my life. I pray that you will be with me today."

His thoughts turned to Russia, wishing that he had received news from Gregori.... Gregori had become a brother to him and he wished he could be there, for the wedding.

His thoughts were interrupted by a commotion at the entrance gate to the garden. The private security men who had been hired to make sure the week of their wedding was as perfect as possible and free of anti-semitic protests, were detaining a man at the gate.

The Russian voice drifting up to his balcony sounded very familiar; "David Weis! Tell these fools to let me in. I am your best friend, or did you forget?"

Gregori Mikhalov shouted, in Russian, at the top of his voice, as he climbed on top of the taxi so that his message would reach the house.

Smiling from ear to ear, David leapt from the short balcony to the path below. Running to the gate.

David shouted back; "Gregori! Gregori! My friend! Gregori I am so happy that you are here!"

The gate opened and the two friends hugged and kissed each other after such a long separation. Judith ran from the house to see what all the noise was about. She realised upon seeing their guest, that this must be the famous Gregori Mikhalov who David told her about. She welcomed him with her hands extended and a smile on her face. Gregori, not knowing the Jewish customs, grabbed her by the waist and twirled her around and kissed her cheeks.

And said, in Russian;"You are absolutely gorgeous! I want to marry you! David you are such a lucky man."

Judith, completely out of balance at Gregori's physical greeting, blushed and stammered. David laughed at the sight of his future bride's muteness.

After regaining her composure, Judith came between both men and hooked an arm with each of them. Turning toward the house, using David to interpret for her, she said; "Gregori, I can never express how thankful I am. We owe you everything. It is wonderful that we can be all together for our wedding! Let's go inside and let me introduce you to the family."

A few hours later.....Putting on her wedding dress, Judith felt like she was having a nervous breakdown. In tears, she was looking at herself in the mirror, wearing her deceased sister's Miriam, wedding dress. She remembered the day when she went with her sister to choose this dress for her wedding to Ezra, David's brother. Miriam let Judith pick the dress for her, telling her, she will be next to be wear it. Lydia, her mother, echoed her loud crying, while holding onto her daughter.

Judith's best friend, and maid of honor, broke the drama exclaiming; "Hey! Today is one of the most important days of your life! I am sure Miriam is smiling on you from above..... The hurts of the past can make you bitter or better, the past is past! Thank God for the newness of today! Look at you two! Red eyes, red noses, makeup running all over your faces. We better hurry up if you want to be married today, or did you change your mind?"

Lydia looking in the mirror said; "we are a mess! "

Two more bridesmaids hurried in to help fix Judith's and Lydia's makeup.

Jacques, Judith's father, trying to find out what was going on, attempted to enter the room only to be pushed out of the door. He reluctantly sat in a hall chair and waited. A few minutes seemed like hours. Chaim, David's father, came to see what the delay was.

He sat down by Jacques and asked him; "It looks like the war didn't touch your house."

Jacques reply, "The Nazi took it for their headquarters. Fortunately, Lydia the girls and I were able to escape to our cottage in Switzerland before the invasion. It was devastating to see the city when we returned. We were expecting our home to be destroyed. When we came down the street and saw our house was still here, we wept with joy. Since the Nazi's occupied this house and did who knows what, I will have no regrets once we find a place in Israel to move to."

Chaim responded; ''Jacques! You are a fantastic architect and Sarai and I have twenty acres of land in Israel. You and Lydia can build a home anywhere on our property. That way we can truly be a family. God willing, our future grandchildren can visit us both without any problem.

''Jacques appreciative, ''This is a perfect solution! I accept with joy!''

Just then the door opened, and his beautiful wife and radiant daughter appeared.

The fragrance of a thousand light pink and white roses filled the garden. A light breeze and the sun's warmth welcomed the guests. The ceremony was to be performed in the Belford's gardens. The spring flowers completed the perfect picture for David and Judith's special day. David was standing in the gazebo. The Rabbi, a non- traditional reformed Jew and a very close friend of Jacques and his family, was chosen to perform the ceremony. David stood there, looking superb in his black tuxedo, making a lot of girls envious of Judith. Finally to David's great relief, the music started. Jacques appeared with Judith at his side. He held Judith's arm and hand very tightly. David's first look at Judith made his heart race. She looked like an empress, so beautiful. Jacques walked Judith down the aisle very slowly on purpose. This was his only daughter, his only child.

The Rabbi said; "Who gives this bride?"

Jacques with emotion, hardly could articulate; "Her father."

He was still tightly holding her arm and hand, when Judith kissed him, and said; "Dad? Let go of my arm."

She almost had to wrestle herself from his grip. In doing so, she walked on her dress and fell to her knees in front of David.

David smiling, helped her up; "Please don't, I am only a human."

Everybody laughed and the tension was broken. Sarai, David's mother played " Handel's Alleluia." The audience was transported to a dreamland. No one in the audience, not even Judith and her parent's, had expected such a great virtuoso to be in their midst. David's heart filled with pride for his mother. It was the first time he had heard his mother play since they lived in Moscow. He jumped from the platform at the end of the piece and hugged his mother and kissed her.

When the time came for them to say their vows, they held hands, a long satin blue ribbon tied around their hands together. Eyes embracing each other, said in one voice; "As long as I live, I will hold your hand. If I go first, I will wait at the gate for you, then we will walk together holding hands forever."

At the end of the ceremony, David broke the traditional glass with his heel. Everybody shouting " Mazel tov!!!"

During the reception, Chaim and Sarai interrupted the festivities. They brought forth a rectangular, blue velvet box inscribed in silver with the couple's names and wedding date.

David and Judith, opened the box and they both gasped in surprise at what was inside. Two silver bar Kochba Shekels were nestled within the silver lining along with a certificate of provenance. Then Jacques and Lydia presented their wedding gift to David and Judith. A leather suitcase which contained two travel vouchers to Israel, including a three week stay at a first class hotel in Jerusalem.

After the reception, Lydia and Sarai accompanied Judith to her room, to help her change into her traveling clothes and to pack.

Sarai with emotion said to Lydia; "Thank you for allowing us to stay another month with you and Jacques. Chaim is so excited about going to the racetrack to Longchamp with Jacques. That's all he talk's about! "

Lydia laughed; "Yes that seems to be all they can talk about! We will let the men do what they want to. Meanwhile, there is that new exhibition of impressionism in that gallery I love, near the Louvre. We also have reservations, to the Paris Opera where Maria Callas is performing."

Judith listened as the women spoke, happy to see them becoming such good friends.

Lydia handed a package to Judith; "Do you want me to put this on the top of your clothes, or under?"

Judith opened the package and blushed as she took out beautiful white satin lingerie. She answered; "I will pack this myself, thank you mother! Sarai I am so sorry that I will miss your recital that mother has planned. It meant so much to David and me that you played at our wedding. That was such a great gift for us !"

Chapter 10

ISRAEL

From the portal of the airplane David and Judith watched as Israel came into view, their hearts beating faster with excitement of being in the land of their ancestors. During their honeymoon, they visited Israel.

One day walking in the old town of Jerusalem, they stopped to admire, a beautiful house. It had a courtyard, which looked like a heavenly garden with majestic plants and abundant flowers. Anna, a widow, was the owner, she was cutting some flowers to put in her vase. She was happy to invite them to visit the inside of the house. It was absolutely Judith's dream of a home with marble columns and a fountain. Anna told them, she put the house up for sale since her husband was kill by the terrorists and that she wanted to move to America to live with her son, a surgeon.

David and Judith bought the house.

After they finished furnishing their house, Judith applied for government work, in the communications field and David joined the Israeli army. After basic training, David was accepted for training in Israel's Special Forces. His abilities were apparent and as he became more proficient in the Hebrew language, he was promoted to captain. David was sent to Farsi and Urdu language schools and to military intelligence gathering training. He was trained in Islamic religion, its cults and propaganda. David was then placed into a Special Forces unit that gathered intelligence in the Arab nation.

Chapter 11

THE MARKETPLACE

What a brew-ha-ha filling the marketplace in Jerusalem! The sun was high, covered by a white cloud. The sounds of the crowd, mainly women and children, were very loud with excited voices bargaining for goods. A group of teenagers, on the corner of a large space near the food market were laughing and playing soccer. The irresistible aroma of cookies filled with honey baked out in the open, permeated Captain David Weis nostrils as he watched from a distance. The smell was so appealing he couldn't resist wandering in that direction. His motion was arrested by the vision of a graceful beautiful lady, almost floating instead of walking, in a gray silk dress that just skimmed her ankles. Her long curly black hair danced with every step she took. Her face alit with a smile in his direction. David thought, what an enchanting vision! Judith, her brown eyes shining upon him, was suddenly thrown into his arms by an enormous explosion. They both fell to the ground. Judith was covered with dust and blood. David shouted from beneath; ''Are you hurt?''

People were screaming and crying in the chaos. Judith put her right hand over her bloody left shoulder. She grabbed hold of a dismembered arm that had landed upon them and flung it aside in horror. Judith astonished said; "No that isn't my blood. Are you injured?" David shook his head no. They rushed to the center of the commotion to aid the victims.

David furious; "How can you stop those things happening when you can't discern between your brother and your enemy?"

As the sun set, David arrived home and immediately washed the day's horrors from his sharply honed body. As David was dressing, he heard the key in the door announcing the arrival of his beloved wife. During the turmoil that followed the marketplace bombing, Judith had accompanied the injured to the hospital.

They hugged, Judith broke their embrace to clean up and prepare the evening's meal consisting of matzo, smoked salmon, dates, figs and jasmine tea. After dinner, they relaxed on the sofa. David closed his eyes and Judith started to massage her husband's body, using lavender oil.

David asks inquisitively; "When will those ignorant fanatics understand that killing innocent people doesn't get you into heaven?'

Judith moved closer to him and put her arms around his neck, caressed his face and raked his short, black curly hair. Judith murmured; "If you die, I die."

David aroused '' I'm not dead yet! So go ahead, love me."

They both rolled from the sofa, on the carpet floor. They knew, from experience, that in this life, every moment counts.

Chapter 12

PROMOTED

Judith earned top security clearance and she transferred to a special unit that controlled the news made available to the Israeli and international media. David progressed through the rank and was looked on by his military superiors and civilian political bosses as a rising star. David and Judith dedicated all their time to their country to make a way for future generations to live safely. Their usual, busy day started by rising at 5 am taking a quick shower followed by breakfast and on the run to martial arts class, then a military history class. After a short lunch, and four hours of linguistics study, Judith would go to work decoding enemy messages and David would report to the base and be on call for military emergencies. Their extremely active lifestyle would have worn out anyone else but their youth and excitement kept them going strong. The only greatest source of entertainment was during the late evening where they could love each other.

So it was natural that nine month later, Judith gave the best gift to David, their first son, Solomon also called Shlomo. The name was chosen, because his parents prayed over him for wisdom. Judith was given leave to nurture and breastfeed her infant. She had never imagined the magical feeling that she felt each time she held her precious son.

In honour of the first born son of any Jewish family, parties take place with all their friends and family during first week of life, followed by the grandest celebration of all which included dancing, feasting and singing.

What a blessing it was to have both Judith and David's parents close by to assist in raising little Shlomo. Sarai, David's mother, would often sit little Shlomo by her side as she played piano and spoke Russian to him. As soon as he was able to sit by himself, he began to play ''duets'' with his grandmother which brought Sarai, and Chaim, great joy and laughter. Judith's parents, Jacques and Lydia, also doted on their grandson. When Shlomo was about two years old, Lydia stopped by Jacques's studio and when she opened the door to his workroom she couldn't help but laugh aloud at the sight that met her eyes.

Lydia joyful; "What are you doing? Are you planning to build our Paris neighbourhood here in Israel?'

Looking up from the miniature model of the neighbourhood in which Judith grew up, including miniature cars, and signs printed in French.

Jacques jubilant; ''Voila! What do you think of this? I can hardly wait to see Shlomo's face when he sees this!''

Lydia amused, ''Mmm...... Are you trying to compete with Sarai?''

Jacques complacent; ''Not exactly....But Shlomo must one day learn to make a living. Music is fine but only a few can feed a family with it!''

After two years, at the great satisfaction of the grandparents, Shlomo was gifted with a little brother, Ezekiel, whom they nicknamed Zeke, who looked very much like his brother except instead of black hair like Shlomo he had red hair.

Judith overwhelmed, ''I always wanted a baby with red hair.''

She began to softly sing; ''La Berceuse de Mozart.'' (Mozart Lullaby)

Chapter 13

SIX YEARS LATER...

David was talking on the phone; "No, can Morris do it ? I have an obligation this afternoon to take my son to soccer practice. Every Tuesday he counts on me..... Mmm, Okay, I will be there in five minutes."

David walked to Judith's office and asked her to take Zeke to soccer practice that afternoon. Judith usually took Shlomo to his music lessons while David took Zeke to soccer practice. She arranged for Lydia, her mother to take Shlomo to his lessons.

Zeke was so excited to have his mother watch him play for a change. Zeke, six years old, vowed to play extra special to make his mother proud. He ran fast, made a goal, and smiled, pointing a finger in his mother's direction, he blew her a kiss, and yelled; "For you Mom!" He finished off his dedication to her with a cartwheel.

Judith laughed so much, to see that every time Zeke took the ball and scored, he repeated this grand gesture to her.

Judith radiated with pride for her son. It surely was an unforgettable afternoon. Zeke's team won the match 5-2,The team carried Zeke across the field on their shoulder's, chanting and cheering, " Zeke! Zeke! Zeke!" for his contribution of 4 of the 5 goals. Normally David would take Zeke and his four friends to the local cafe for a cold lemonade and a small ice cream. In order to celebrate this victory, Judith allowed the boys to order large ice creams along with their cold drinks.

The youngsters were full of joy and bragged to one another about their heroic efforts on the field that day, eating their delicious ice cream.

Judith amused said; "Alright boys! Behave, I am going to the lady's restroom."

As she was combing her hair, smiling at the memory of the day's events, she felt the room shake and immediately heard an all too familiar sound of an explosion.

She ran to where their table had been. The sight that met her eyes made her heart stop. Zeke and his friends lay on the floor in large puddles of blood. Judith immediately dropped to her knees and started CPR on Zeke and continued until the ambulances, arrived. One boy died at the scene, Zeke and the other boys were rushed to the hospital in critical condition.

The criminal was a 13-year-old Palestinian boy, dressed in soccer team clothing. He had walked amongst the six outdoor tables and had blown himself up with explosives strapped to his waist. One observer reported that he had smiled and yelled; "For Allah!".

Judith sat numbly as the surgeon pronounced his verdict. Zeke had lost one leg and both of his eyes. The surgeon did not think Zeke would make it through the night. David rushed to the hospital as soon as he heard of the tragedy, not knowing whether Judith and Zeke had been there or not.

As soon as he rounded the corner in the emergency area, his heart fell as he saw Judith kneeling next to the bed where his son lay.

The doctor stopped David and gave him the news. As David came closer he saw tears in Judith eyes and the soft, broken words of "La Berceuse de Mozart", Judith singing in French close to Zeke's ear. "sleep quietly,... the blue night cast out the sun...., the dream under your closed eyes....., may come and caress your rest......., it is a blond angel........ watching near your forehead......., he will give you a happy dream....., sleep my darling child sleep."

David gently held his son's hand, kissed him, and whispered; "I love you" in Zeke's ear.

Judith kept hers eyes closed and re-lived every moment of joy, that had happened that afternoon at soccer practice. David did not want to interrupt Judith's dream world, so he prayed for strength. He did not know what to do with Judith. She was still there on her knees, with her eyes closed and a smile on her face, watching Zeke, running, laughing, his young voice shout, "For you Mom!" and blowing her a kisses over and over again. She wanted to stay in the soccer field with Zeke, forever and never move from that spot.

David gathered Judith into his arms. She opened her eyes with regret, and held him so tightly he felt her fingernails into his flesh. She buried her head into his neck and sobbed, "No, no, oh no!" David cradled her like a baby, and whispered in her ear, "sh, sh, sh, sh" as he used to do to comfort his own children.

Trembling, Judith's voice was very weak, she said; "Thank God it was me, who went to the soccer practice today. Otherwise I would have lost both my husband and my son. I was in the ladies room when the explosion happened."

David held her tighter and was grateful for Judith's vanity. For fixing her lipstick and combing her hair had saved her life. Together, they held their son as he drew his last breath of life.

Although David dealt with death and dying every day, he had never experienced the pain of losing a child. It was indescribable. The pain was so brutal he had to get away. David kissed his son and then kissed the top of Judith's head as she wept over Zeke's bed.

He hurried outside to the hospital's garden courtyard. He fell to his knees behind a bush, in mourning, he pled to God; "O God, Please, please take the pain away! .... Death! You win again! God if you are real, what do you want me to do? Where are your blessings? What have I done wrong?!"

David, suddenly felt a soft hand upon his shoulder, looking up he saw a lady, the sun was shining in her face. Intrigued he asked; "Are you an angel?"

She answered; "I volunteer at the hospital, and when I heard about the bombing, I came to the ER. I am Elisabeth Bloomberg. My husband and my four children were kill in the market place explosion, caused by Muslim terrorists two years ego. I was in the ER when they brought your son in accompanied by your wife. I believe God put me here, at this time and in this place to help you in your grief. I saw your wife, for a very brief moment, she looked like a friend I had in La Sorbonne in Paris, Judith Bedford."

David surprised; "She is Judith, your friend, I remember her telling me about you Elisabeth!"

For an instant David's mind was distracted from its grief, thinking about Judith's surprise to reconnect with her old friend.

Elisabeth moved with compassion and said; "Can I come tonight to help Judith and the family prepare Zeke for the funeral?"

David grateful said; "Please come. To see you again will bring comfort to Judith's heart."

When Judith saw Elisabeth, they hugged and cried together, holding each other for a long time. After supper Judith and Elisabeth retired to the living room. They sat on the sofa Elisabeth said; "Judith you remember, I was an atheist, but my husband was a religious Jew, so I converted, and we brought up our children in the Jewish faith. When my husband died a few hours after our children died, his last words were; "Jesus is the Christ". I was perplexed. The volunteer next to his bed was a Christian. He told me that before I got there, he and my husband had prayed together. The volunteer then told me that my loved ones were in a much better place and he tried to comfort me.

The man's name was Paul and his wife Kira. They took me under their wings and prayed over me. They fed me physically and spiritually. After my family perished, there were times of bitterness and fear accompanied by drinking and using pain killers. My husband's revolver, was a great temptation.

One day I put it against my head and when I pulled the trigger, it got jammed. In rage, I threw the revolver and it went off putting a hole in the chair. I grabbed the revolver again, and put it in my mouth using my two hands to pull the trigger.

It jammed again. The door bell rang, I did not close the door. Paul and his wife Kira came in, very concerned. They put the revolver away and told me; "Elisabeth God loves you so much, you must believe that he loves you!"

I became hysterical, Yes God loves me so much that he killed my parents, my husband and my four children! Yes that is love? WHY ! WHY ! WHY! I cried for a long time, like a badly wounded animal. In a soft gentle voice, Kira said, we learned from a very ancient book, even before Abraham. The book of Enoch. Enoch never died, he was elevated to heaven, just like the prophet Elijah. Enoch reported during his life time, he was devoted to praises and talking with God.

One day God let him see in the spirit, the past and the future. When God created all things including the angels, and other humans. He give's them free will, to love Him and serve Him.

Lucifer was the most talented and beautiful of all the angels. Everyone in heaven admired him, he became so proud. Some will be completely taken by his beautiful voice and music.

Lucifer started to use his power. Then Lucifer (Satan) decided to be God. It was a war in heaven. Michael and Gabriel and the faithful angels of God fought against Lucifer and his army and cast them to the earth.

Many years later, God created the garden of Eden with Adam and Eve...... They disobeyed and were cast out from the garden of Eden.

Their two sons were brought up in the fear of the Lord. Cain's jealousy over Abel led him to kill his brother.

The Lord said, "What have you done? Your brother's blood cries out to me. You are banished from the ground you have defiled with your brother's blood. From now on you will be a fugitive on the earth. Cain replied; "My punishment is too great for me to bear. All who see me will try to kill me."

Cain went to the land of Nod, and took a wife."

I said; "Please Kira STOP! You annoy me with your Bible story."

Kira paused and said; That is to confirm, humans were already living there. But not many people know the writing of Enoch, only what we learn in the Bible which say's Enoch was the seventh generation after Adam. And Enoch lived in close relationship with God.

Many scientists speculate that we are descendant's of an extinct species or race of human beings called, Homo Neanderthalensis ...... But when we know God, we know all the evil on earth comes from our free will, and Satan who lies, destroys and kills.

God's love is pure and perfect, He give us the best of Himself, his only beloved son, for whoever believes in Him will be saved and have everlasting life if we choose Him."

I told her; "Here you go again..."

She said to me; "Elisabeth, you must ask Jesus to reveal himself to you. You will be born again, you will have peace."

One night I screamed in desperation; "Jesus help me!" I cried very loud, lying in my bed in the dark room.....

Suddenly a bright light came over me, and a man's voice said; "Here I am, you are precious to me, come to me, and I will give you peace. Not the kind of peace like the world gives."

I was completely taken by the vision, this glorious man. Jesus had actually appeared to me. It was like living in a different dimension. The pain was gone, and I know now with certainty, my beloved is know in a better place than this one. I was free from my tormented spirit."

Judith was listening to the comforting words of her dearest friend, and said; "I wish that the pain in my heart would stop, I cannot accept not to see my little boy anymore, this is pure torture.... ….......But Elisabeth you said everyone who believes in Jesus would have everlasting life. We don't believe in Jesus neither did Zeke..... So where is he?"

Elisabeth, her arms around Judith answered her; "Children are too young to decide. ….Jesus said; "let the little children come to me, for of such is the Kingdom of heaven!" ...Judith, let's close our eyes together, please take some deep breaths. Now imagine Zeke running and playing with his friends full of joy in the Kingdom of heaven.

For you to be together in heaven for ever, you must pray something like this; "Jesus I don't know you, but I need you. Please help me to believe.... Just pray whatever comes from your heart."

Elisabeth kissed her, then stood up and left the room. Lydia and Sarai were with Shlomo, crying and holding him. Elisabeth prayed over them, then suggested for them to convince David and Judith to take a break and to go to Paris for two weeks or so.

Ten days later, Lydia and Jacques, came home with a smile on their face. David and Judith had stayed with them since Zeke died.

Lydia tenderly said; " We have a gift for you two, two weeks in Paris first class ticket, at the Hotel Ritz. You are going next Thursday."

David and Judith looked at her in stupor, then their thoughts went to Paris, were they first meet, and "La Sorbonne with all their friends, all the places where they walked together and fell in love.

David said; "We are so very grateful. Thank you so much.."

Lydia continued; "Hanukkah, the feast of lights, is December 23rd this year. It will be less painful for us and Shlomo, we can imagine that you are in Paris with Zeke, and enjoying yourselves. December in Paris with all the streets and shops illuminated to celebrate Christmas, will remind you of the beautiful time you had in Paris with all your friends."

Chapter 14

BACK TO PARIS

Judith did not lose contact with her favourite friends. Miriam, Bethany, Sarah, Esther and Alex. They all came to the airport to welcome them, with flowers, Esther played her violin. They had a huge sign; ''WELCOME BACK DAVID AND JUDITH!!!''

This warm welcome brought laughter to David and Judith's hearts. The hotel room was luxurious with big fresh flowers and a bottle of champagne with caviar was waiting for them. To be in the atmosphere of Paris. Really helped the mood. December in Paris was like a fairy tale; Just when they arrived, the snow started to put a shining white blanket on the streets and trees, with Christmas music playing on every street, it was magical.

The hotel was richly decorated for the biggest party of the year. David and Judith holding hands, walked in the street at evening were taken with the aroma of chestnuts grilled out in the open on charcoal. David bought a big brown paper cone filled with hot chestnuts.

Judith appreciative, voiced; "Almost ten years since we did have that!"

They walked, admiring the shops with their enchanting displays of the miniature village of Bethlehem. One very nicely decorated book store called, "Le Grenier" (The Attic) was Judith's favorite place when she was young. Inside you climb ancient stone stairs going up to the Attic where there was a story teller for children.

Judith suddenly said; "Let's go listen to the story."

Coming from the attic, the lovely voice of the story teller was familiar to Judith's ears. She whispered surprised; "I cannot believe it! this is Madame Marguerite my ballet teacher! When I was ten years old, my mother wanted my sister and I to take ballet class in order to have better posture and be more graceful. I was a real Tomboy"

David smiled, "You Judith a Tomboy? Very hard to believe!"

They sat in the back with the children's parents.

Judith interested; "I am surprised she will read a Christmas story, because she is a Jew. Her real name is Sarah Hoffman, but because of prejudice she changed her name to Marguerite Desly to be accepted in the Opera of Paris. She was a prima ballerina."

Marguerite captivated her young audience, telling the story of "The Christmas Star" in a theatrical way. The story was about....... A little boy Eric, asking "Grandmother why did we put a star on top of the tree?" The Grandma started;

"Once upon a time a long long long time ago. There was a star shinning more than every other star. This very special star's name was "Magic." Why Magic? Because this star had special power. Magic can go all over the world very fast:

ZOOM ! ZOOM ! ZOOM! In the night, and can see all the world's children. The good ones, who did their prayers and obeyed their parents, and the naughty ones, who pretended to go to sleep and snuck out of the window through the night, to meet other naughty children and do bad things. Magic will see so many people fighting, screaming at each other, and some very mean. Magic was sad, he wanted the world to have joy and to love each other.

Magic went to talk to his father, the King of the stars. He said; "I want to see people happy just like us, full of light and peace" The King said; "What do you plan to do about that?" Magic answered; "I have an idea, you are the King of the Universe......so you can make me to be born like one of them, and....and... I will change the world."

The King was laughing; "To be born like a human baby?"

Magic enthusiastic; "Yes! so they will understand me, please father let me do that. I want to do something big, that the whole world will rejoice for ever!"

The King was thinking, then... he said; "That is a noble idea but for you to be born a human, you need a mother, you must find a very special young lady with a pure heart. I don't think you can find anyone on earth with a pure heart."

Magic optimistic responded; "Father, I am going to search the earth to find my mother to be."

ZOOM ZOOM ZOOM!

Magic found many beautiful girls and princesses, but they did not have a pure heart.

ZOOM ! ZOOM! ZOOM! Magic went to Israel, He stopped with surprise. There was a young lady looking up at the stars in the sky, her name was Mary, she was singing. "

When I wish upon a star....all my heart is full of joy!....la la la la la!" Magic saw her heart was pure!

ZOOM! ZOOM! ZOOM! Magic was back to his father, very excited .

Magic exultant said; "I found my mother! Her name is Mary! Look down right there, here she is! So sweet and beautiful with a pure heart!"

His father the king was sad to let Magic go for so long. Magic promised; "I will be back, and be with you for ever, after I accomplished my goal."

His father blessed him with favor to heal the world.

Mary married Joseph, and they where going to Bethlehem, to see important people.

One special beautiful night, all the stars in the sky started to sing:

"Joy to the world The king is born! To bring peace and love and joy! Joy! Joy! Joy!"

Magic was born a human, his name was JESUS.

Jesus grew to be the most popular boy in all the world, healing broking hearts, and every sickness and every infirmity. After many years Jesus finished his goal on earth, he went back to his father the King.

That is why we put a star on the top of the tree. THE END!"

All the children's applauded. They asked their parents to buy the book, and have Madame Marguerite sign her book.

David bought one for his son, and asked Madame Marguerite to dedicated the book to Shlomo. She lifted her head, smiled and said: "Shalom." Judith grab her hand exclaiming; "Madame Marguerite! You were my ballet teacher long ago, do you remember me, Judith Bedford?"

Marguerite surprised; "Judith! of course I remember you! Where have you been all these years?"

Judith introducing David, answered her; "I am married to David we live in Israel with our parents."

Marguerite; "Dear, dear, with all those terrorists? It is a dangerous place to live... Please come tomorrow at 3 pm, here is my address we need to talk."

The next day, David and Judith arrived at 3 pm, bringing flowers and a box of chocolate.

A nice looking old gentleman opened the door to welcome them. He introduced himself; "I am Daniel I consider myself the most lucky man on earth, to be the husband of the delightful Marguerite.

Come on in, she is preparing her favorite cake, the famous Pavlova."

Marguerite appeared with her arms opened to hug and kiss Judith and David.

Marguerite elated said; " What a wonderful pleasant surprise to see you again after so many years."

Judith told her the story of her life, with the last tragedy about Zeke.

Marguerite sat between Judith and David on the sofa and closed her eyes, and held Judith and David's hand. Daniel came and put his hands on their shoulders.

Marguerite moved with compassion prayed; "Lord, there is no word to comfort in a tragedy like this, but only You Jesus can heal those wounded parents. Please Lord, with your love, touch them, they need You! Thank You Lord."

Strangely Judith felt a warmth inside of her, she thought, it's like being with Elisabeth.

Judith wiping her tears finally said; "Madame Marguerite you don't teach ballet anymore? Why?"

Marguerite replied; "I am 64 and last year my husband fell down and broke his hip. I tried to help him to get up to sit on a chair. You can see Daniel is much taller than I am. I fractured my back doing so. For two months I was not able to walk. My assistant Irina a young Russian lady, is an excellent ballet teacher, I gave her the academy. ….…..But all is well as I find so much joy reading stories to children in Le Grenier (the attic).

Judith could not resist to ask; "But Madame Marguerite, I remember you to be a Jew, but you pray to Jesus, why?"

Marguerite smile pointing to Daniel. "When the war started in Romania, Daniel flew with his parents to Australia. He is a well educated man who is related to king Michael the First of Romania. Daniel decided to be a crocodile hunter for the skin, and to trap venomous snakes alive for the serum laboratory to produce anti-venom. He lived in the jungle for two years, with another crazy young man named John, together risking their lives.

One day in an Aboriginal village, a couple of missionaries were ministering to the people. One young woman died after giving birth. A French missionary lady prayed over the dead woman with authority and commanded to the evil spirit of death to come out of her body. The missionary was yelling at the evil spirit. It was like a spiritual battle was going on. …..… Then the woman opened her eyes, sat up, and said: "I am hungry." The whole village accepted Jesus Christ as their Lord, and Daniel did too. …..…..Then Daniel came with his family to live in Paris. One day he came in my ballet class to pick up his young sister Marjorie. The way he looked at me, made me uncomfortable. He was in his 40's and I was too. He came back three times a week to pick up Marjorie and would sometimes stay during the class. After class he would talk to me. I asked him if he had a job to go to, instead of staying to watch the class? He said yes, but he works only in the mornings. I was suspicious, and asked, what kind of job is that? He answer, I teach biology at the university La Sorbonne. I was impressed. …...He always had a Bible with him, which I mocked him about it. He just smiled and said; "One day you will love this book as your life depends on it." Inquisitive, after class we went to a Tea room to talk. He told me his story in the jungle, where he went from being an atheist to become a christian. I started laughing and said; are you for real? He took my hand looked at me in the eyes, and said; "I want to marry you and you are going to say yes, because God told me you are my wife to be."

I was stunned, I became red, and lost my speech. I released my hand from his grip and ran away as fast as my legs could run. I think I broke the track record that day. Two months later we got married. I can sincerely say at 64 years old, I am so blessed, God gave me a man who adores me, even with my old face and body, he calls me "beautiful". Daniel always sees good things in me and encourage's me to write books. My heart is full of thanksgiving to my Lord for giving me such a precious life in my old age."... Marguerite stand up and went to the kitchen.

Daniel continued the conversation; "What Marguerite did not tell you, was when she ran away, I ran after her. I saw her entering an old theatre damaged by WW2 with a big sign that said, "Welcome," so I went in, the lobby was packed with hundred's of young people. I asked, do you know Madame Marguerite?

And a group answered; "Yes she is our Queen mother!" Marguerite appeared and said; "Here are all my children!"

I asked how many are you? One person responded 109! Marguerite was laughing, telling me; " To marry me, that means you must marry all of us!" I responded, 109 hum?...... is not a good number for me...............What about 110? I went on my knees and asked; "Marguerite will you marry me? After a couple of minutes, she said "YES.".......... Marguerite is the only person I know, who did what Jesus said to do, in Matthew: "I was hungry and you gave me food; I was thirsty and you gave me drink; I was a stranger and you took me in; I was naked and you clothed me; I was sick and you visited me; I was in prison and you came to me. I said to you, in as much as you did it to one of the least of these, you did it to me." That day Marguerite became my hero! She gave all her fortune to provide for the homeless. ....She invited both of you only for tea at 3pm, because from 8 am to 2 pm we are in the theater every day."

David and Judith where astonished. David asked; "Can we visit your theater, and give you a hand?"

"Absolutely, responded Daniel, what about 9 am tomorrow? Here is the address."

Marguerite arrived from the kitchen with a large silver tray, with the spectacular "Pavlova."

Marguerite put the tray on the table;

"You probably know that Anna Pavlova, was a famous Russian prima ballerina in 1881-1931 Her favorite treat was meringue with whip cream and raspberry on top. To honour her memory they called this desert, "Pavlova" and it is our favorite too!."

David and Judith were also captivated with the delicious "Pavlova."

Chapter 15

JUST A LITTLE SIP

Back at their hotel, they started to get ready to have dinner with their friends from the University in Montmartre, where they used to go together when they where students.

Their friends were already there. Bethany was with her husband Alex, who was the best man with Gregori at their wedding. Esther and Sarah came also with their husbands. Miriam was a widow. Her husband died three years before in a car accident.

They were waiting for David and Judith with an opened bottle of Cabernet Sauvignon wine, and Brie cheese with the French baguette.

They put a glass of wine in David's and Judith's hand and sang together the French song; "Drink a little sip it's so pleasant, but just a little sip, just a little sip, so you will not became foolish, drink a little sip.....just a little sip....To celebrate friendship!"

They all hugged and kissed. Then each one shared their story's, eating steak, fries and salad. Just like in the old days.

David and Judith forgot their sorrow for a little while. Walking back to their hotel with a smile on their face. Since Zeke died this was the first time, they enjoyed the day and had a good night's sleep.

Next morning, they arrived at the theater 9 am sharp. Everyone shouted "WELCOME HOME!" David and Judith brought a huge basket of 250 warm croissants, with jam and butter. After breakfast, they moved inside the theater where people were rehearsing their part of the play. Marguerite directed and Daniel was doing the narrative.

Daniel told David and Judith; "Every day they all take a chapter of the Bible and make it a living play, so everyone is memorising the word with pleasure."

David and Judith were very surprised to see people improvising with songs and music. Thirty people were playing instruments. It was a real professional concert.

Curious, Judith asked Daniel, "Where did all those talented people come from?"

Daniel answered; "Some from Romania, fleeing for their lives when the communists took over. Others came from Paris, who had played in the orchestra but lost their job during WW2. Some Jews from Germany who came back from the concentration camps had lost everything, family and homes. They were sitting in the street with no hope, left in despair. Marguerite would sit with them and cry with them. She told them, I don't have children, will you please be my children? She took them, cleaned them up, put clothes on their backs............All those kids, well some are older than you. For us they are our kids. That doesn't mean we don't have problems, every family has some, but we surrender to the Lord all our burden's. Every Sunday at 5 pm we have a play opened to the public, with no charge. We have three wooden boxes in the lobby for volunteer offering. Most of the time we have more money coming in than if we charged for a ticket. Every body works on stage or behind the stage. Decors, costumes, lights, special equipment for the flying angels, all made by them,"

Judith surprised, " You have flying angels? You really mean flying? How do you do that?"

Daniel said, "We have acrobats and trapeze artists from a Romanian circus that burned down during the revolution."

Judith asks; " If Jesus Christ is the Jewish Messiah, why do Christians want to kill us?"

Daniel was pleased to answer her; "Men wants to be in charge. They create a God according to their image. Jesus came to reveal the character of God His Father, loving and merciful. God who created the world with people of every nationality and colour, just want everyone to be saved! Men are prejudiced. God gives us free will to choose to obey him, or reject him. God is love. If we don't love people, that means we don't know God. Those who call themselves Christian and hate the creation of God are not Christian. That is what ignorant, full of hatred people do. They don't know the scriptures, or they twist the word of God to do their own will."

Judith liked very much Daniel's explanation. She said; "What you just said makes sense. My friend Elisabeth believes in Jesus, but it was those who call themselves christian, who killed her parents. She said, I don't want to call myself, "Christian," instead I call myself, "A complete Jew, because I know Jesus is my Jewish Messiah."

It was late and the street with all the lights and Christmas decorations was so beautiful, David and Judith decided to walk back to the hotel.

David told Judith; "I like my Jewish religion, that is the one I embrace and love because of you and your parents. Judaism is the right religion, because the Messiah is a Jew, and I will stay faithful to it. If Jesus is the Jewish Messiah, there is no reason for me to change religion, it is just to accept what was promised to us, by the prophet Isaiah saying to our fathers:

> *"Hearing you will hear and shall not understand, and seeing you will see and not perceive. For the heart of this people has grown dull. Their ears are hard of hearing; Their eyes have closed; Lest they should see with their eyes and hear with their ears; Lest they should understand with their heart and turn, so that I should heal them."*

Judith was on the phone speaking to Esther, about Madame Marguerite and her husband. Esther also used to go to Madame Marguerite's dance classes.

Esther jubilant; "I would love to go Sunday to see the performance in the theater, I am going to ask our friends to come with us."

Sunday they all met in the lobby of the Ritz hotel. Then they went to the theater to meet Madame Marguerite and her husband Daniel.

What a joyful reunion! Alex was one of Daniel's students in biology at La Sorbonne. They all sat with Daniel in the balcony. Marguerite went behind the stage to direct everything.

The curtain opened with the symphony of Handel's "Messiah" with a choir of 30 voices, all dressed in blue costumes covered with shining stars. Seven ballerinas were dancing on their toes, like they where floating in perfect harmony, disappearing in the dark blue sky. Three kings on their camels entered the scene in regal costumes. The three tenor "kings" were singing; "Amazing Grace." Then four shepherds came in playing flutes and singing, with six little lambs. The three kings were singing back to them asking the shepherds; "Where! Where Is the new born king? Where?! Where is the new born king?"

Their voices amazed the crowd. Judith and her friends stared with their mouths open in surprise.

They asked Daniel; "From where do those tenors come from?"

Daniel replied; "They are from the Opera of Paris. They are volunteering to perform for the month of December until Christmas. We are good friends."

Then the curtain came down. A young lady violinist on toe shoes, dressed like Mozart, started playing Mozart Minuet on her violin while dancing with the blue velvet curtain behind her.

Then the curtain opened. The background décor was the valley of Bethlehem. Two black Arabian horses were ridden by acrobats dressed as gladiators. They were performing on the horses picking shiny scarfs off the ground, then standing on the top of the horses in perfect balance, going fast in circles crossing each other. It was exciting to watch!

David intrigued asked Daniel; "Where do you keep those horses, camels, and sheep?"

"A lot of people ask me the same question." Daniel responded; "During the revolution in Romania, the circus people ran for their lives on camels and horses. They arrived near Paris. A dairy farmer with big pasture gave them hospitality in exchange for working at his farm. The farmer and his three sons are the singing shepherds in the show. They are also good friends and they bring the animals every Sunday to perform."

The curtain came down, and a juggler came to the front of the curtain to entertain until they changed scenery. Then the curtain opened.

The orchestra played; "Joy to the world" with five angels flying and singing.

The live Nativity scene was out of this world! It sounded as if the entire audience synchronistically exclaimed "Wow!" The shepherds with their lambs, the three Kings with their camels, and the acrobat gladiators, with their horses. For the Grand Finale, everyone was on the stage. The whole dark blue background curtain, was full of faces in shining stars, singing all together; "Joy to the world" in perfect harmony.

Then Joseph and Mary stood up. Joseph held the baby, (representing Jesus) right under a shining Star.

The choir became silent and the three kings started to sing "O Holy Night the stars are brightly shining. It is the night of our dear Saviour's birth. Long lay the world in sin and error pining, til He appeared and the soul felt its worth; A thrill of hope the weary world rejoices, for yonder breaks a new and glorious morn. Fall on your knees!....(Then all of those on stage, one after another fell on their knees.) O hear the angel voices! O night divine, O night when Christ was born, O night divine.....O night, O night DIVINE!!!!"

It was sublime. The public gave them a standing ovation.

David was moved and said to Daniel; "Amazing words, so deep. Who wrote those words?"

Daniel responded; "O Holy night, was written by the French poet and author, Placide Cappeau. In 1843 a Parish priest asked him to write a Christmas poem. Cappeau had no interest in religion. Shortly thereafter, Adolphe Adam, who was a prolific French music composer and critic, decided to compose the music. "O Holy Night" and the song became one of the most well known Christmas carols reflecting on Jesus' birth and the redemption of humanity."

Judith with Esther, Myriam, Bethany and Sarah were shouting: "BRAVO! BRAVO ! BRAVO!"

Daniel had disappeared. Then they saw him on stage, with a huge flower bouquet, presenting them to Marguerite the choreographer.

After the show, Daniel and Marguerite, let their people take care of everything. Then they went with their friends to have dinner at "Rigoletto" the Italian restaurant (nearby).

The owner was delighted to see Marguerite and Daniel. He was a faithful visitor to the theater. He insisted on making a feast for them at his expense.

Esther stood up and lifted up her glass of Chianti, and said; "Madame Marguerite you are the lady who will make me dream for a long time with this enchanted evening. Please tell us your Prima ballerina story."

During the dessert and the champagne, Marguerite, after a long sigh, started her story; "I did not become a prima ballerina because I was more talented, no, no, no. I have so many struggles and was the one less likely to make it. My parents were wealthy. My father was the man I admired the most in the whole world. I went to ballet school when I was eight years old. At 13, I got the Poliomyelitis virus, followed by partial paralysis in my left side. My dream to be a ballerina did not go away. For months I asked my mother to take me every day to the Municipal pool. That was my physical therapy. When I was alone I would put on my ballet shoes and would fall down a thousand times but always got up to try again.

Two years later I was back in the ballet school in preparation for the Opera of Paris. My Russian teacher, Cheloudiakoff, was tough but he noticed that I would not give up. My left side was weaker than my right side. I would stay after class for hours working on my handicapped leg. I did not noticed that Professor Cheloudiakoff was observing me. One day he said, "If you want to be chosen, when you are tested to enter the Opera ballet, you need to show your personality, and what you do the best. You have good elevation, so do your special, grand jeté in the air, and double gargouillade." So I worked on my speciality to be spectacular. That was, what opened the door for me. Then my Opera teacher was also Russian, Madame Kousnetzoff, a friend of my previous teacher. She helped me over and over to adjust my left leg. In 1940, my father told me we must all move to America. He feared Hitler may invade France. I refused vehemently to go. So we all stayed in Paris. I bitterly regretted this for ever. When the Nazi invaded Paris. I was in the Opera rehearsing with Madame Kousnetzoff, my ballet teacher. We went hiding, under the theater in a cave. ....The concierge came to bring us food, and told us the horrible news. He did not know I was a Jew.... One day he said, all the Jews were deported, and all their houses and belongings were confiscated by the Nazis. Those who resisted them were shot. All the magnificent paintings and sculptures my father bought were gone. The rich girl I was, became poor. Just like those destitute I had despised in the past since I believed everything was only about me, me who overcame my handicap to become a prima ballerina... But suddenly I became one of them. Later, I learned the Nazi's shot my father. My mother and my young brother died in a concentration camp. At the liberation, the Americans came with food and candies. ….........I felt horribly guilty. If I only had done what my father asked me to do and go with them to America before the war. They would be alive today. My guilt was unbearable until I met Daniel. He introduced me to Jesus Christ.

This is the way it happened I was alone in my room, I was crying until I did not have any more tears. Suddenly a bright light, like a million strings of diamonds was over me and a warm feeling inside of me, washing me, and then Jesus Christ appeared, and He touched me and healed my broken heart."

Everyone sitting at the table was astonished. They all hugged Marguerite and Daniel.

Chapter 16

LOVE IS STRONGER THAN HATE

The next day, with their friends they went to the Opera to see "RIGOLETTO." Daniel's "treat" for all of them. David, Judith and their friends joined Daniel and Marguerite. Together, they arrived early. In the front of the Opera was a commotion. A crowd of journalist's and photographers, were asking question's to a celebrity, a nice tall man was answering them. Everyone was captivated by his radiant face and his eloquence.

Daniel exclaiming; "Wait a minute! That is Richard Wurmbrand! my friend from Romania! Last September he was in the communist prison. The news told us about the Norwegian Christian leaders who paid 10,000 dollars to the communist for his release. I guess after so many years he wanted to celebrate Christmas in Paris with his wife Sabina. She is an excellent speaker. She studied chemistry in Paris at La Sorbonne, when I was there as a student myself. They are both Jews who endured fourteen years of communist imprisonment and torture for their faith in their homeland of

Romania. In 1945 Richard Wurmbrand and his wife Sabina started an "Underground" ministry in Romania for enslaved people and to the invading Russian soldiers. Richard was arrested in 1948, along with his wife Sabina. His wife was a slave labourer for three years on the Danube canal. Only the thought of seeing her son, six year old Mihai Michael, named after our dear king Michael, that gave her the strength to endure the most terrible conditions she was living. She never stopped to witness to everyone she met. Two weeks ago the news reported their stories. Richard testified before the U.S Senate's Internal Security Subcommittee and stripped to the waist to show the scars of eighteen deep torture wounds, covering his torso. His story was carried across the world throughout the U.S Europe and Asia; Richard was warned last September 1966, that the communist regime in Romania planned to assassinate him, yet he would not be silent in the face of a death threat."

Richard Wurmbrand stood out in the crowd, tall and very thin. The journalist asked him; "Do you seek vengeance against those who tortured you?"

Richard answers; "No! You must hate the evil systems, but love your persecutors. Love their souls, for they need Christ. Try to win them to Jesus Christ."

Richard and Sabina finally were able to walk away.

Daniel, being very tall, caught their attention by calling their names and waving. They turned towards his direction and immediately exploded with joy and ran to him to greet him with hugs and kisses. Daniel introduced their nine Jewish friends to them. They all where ecstatic to be with friendly Jews. Sabina joyfully said; "After the performance we must gather together."

Richard and Sabina were sitting in the balcony with King Michael of Romania, who hosted them in his Paris home.

After the show, they all met in the Opera cafeteria. King Michael was pleased to see his cousin Daniel and Marguerite.

Esther and Alex her husband, found a long conference table for all of them in the back room. Everyone gave a short story of their life. Then they all wanted to hear Sabina and Richard's story and asked them, why they accepted to be tortured instead of just flying away to America?

Richard in a tranquil warm voice explained; "Looking back on my life, I am astonished at how much I have been through. More than 30 years have passed since I started the work of preaching the Christian message to the Jews. We Jews don't like to be called "Christian" when we accept Jesus to be the Messiah...But the definition of the word makes sense, if we walk in the steps of Jesus Christ, what do you call it? Christian mean's to try to walk with Christ. If we love God and obey, He will send the Spirit of Truth. That is our choice, to stand for our beliefs no matter the cost, or to retaliate. If I love God above myself and let the Holy Spirit possess me, then I walk in a different dimension, and I can do all with the strength of Jesus."

Judith interrupted;" But, I cannot understand why your face is so..... radiant with joy, after so much tribulation?"

Richard smiled at her and said; "It is the reward to know I bring souls out of hell."

"But why do you want to convert Jews to Christianity? Jews have the right Religion." asked David.

Richard was always stimulated with those kind of questions; "Yes Judaism is the right Religion but Christianity is the right belief. The scriptures teach us that Jesus is the Jewish Messiah."

Then Sarah interjected; "If Christians know that Jesus is the Jewish Messiah, why do they call us "dirty Jews"?"

Sabina chose to answer her; "In Romania, it was a symbol of everything anti-semitic and "Jew" was stamped on our identity cards, as on our hearts, but Richard went from neighbor to neighbor breaking the ice. He had this confidence in his belief that souls can be won to Christ. Richard was not easily discouraged by worldly cynicism or brutality. He could find the right words about the Saviour for different people or warn about the repercussions of living in sin without giving offence. He could charm or cajole, yet be very direct. His blue eyes could look into your soul. Richard went to work strategically, first on our new landlord, trying to bring a humorous approach to something quite touchy.

Mr. Parvalescu, exploded; "You Jews have never done a damned thing that's any good!" Richard who was standing in their parlour, simply replied; "That's a fine sewing machine, what's its make? A Singer! Wasn't that invented by a Jew? Mr. Parvalescu, if you really think the Jews are useless, you'd better get rid of it then"

Across from us was Mrs. Georgescu, who raged about, "those Jews" and soon she was confiding her woes to Richard. Her young son was wild, she feared he would catch a venereal disease. Richard promised to speak to him, and said to her; " But even if he was to catch something, these things can be cured now, although the remedy was invented by a Jew".

"He gradually broke down their prejudice. Then he told them the gospel message. Soon they began to change with new politeness followed by affection. One new friend was a policeman with a motorcycle. He drank and beat his wife, until Richard spoke to him and Christ gave him a new heart.

When air raids began, we couldn't leave the city, Jews were not allowed to travel.

But the policeman took our son, Mihai Michael, out to stay with friends in the country until the worst was over. If they were challenged, Michael was to give them the fine Romanian name of "Jon M. Vlad." Our 6 year old, was thrilled by the adventure."

"I just cannot understand why the whole world hates us so much?" interrupted Bethany.

Richard took over the conversation; "I have endured the heat of the battle in a most important part of the battlefield, where the eternal struggle between light and darkness is waged. The Jews declare daily in their synagogues,

"You have chosen us from among the people." And
Jesus said; "Salvation is from the Jews." John 4:22.

The "dirty Jews" are the cause of all our troubles. Jews around the world have been depicted in literature, some people find in Christianity their true happiness, others hate Christianity and would like to see it destroyed. It is a Jew, Jesus, who is the cause of their happiness or their fury. Some people benefit from capitalism, others feel they are exploited by a capitalist system and would like to see it overthrown. Whether you feel attracted or repelled by capitalism, your attitude will largely be determined by Jews whom you probably have never seen face to face, since the people who have the final say, in the capitalist world, are almost always anonymous. Communism derives from the Jew, Karl Marx, without whom the revolution in the East would have been impossible. The fate of a farmer in Vietnam, who has never seen a Jew in his life will depend on whether he reads the book about the Jew Jesus, or the book about the Jew, Karl Marx. Both are bound up with a jewish name.

Einstein, a Jew, gave the United States a start in atomic weapons. The Jew, Teller, is the father of the nuclear bomb. The Rosenbergs, also Jews, gave atomic secrets to Russia. In scientific books the universe is named after a Jew. We speak of Einstein's Universe, as though we lived in this universe as the guests of a Jew..... ....And this is really so, for we are in fact the guests of a Jew, only his name is not Einstein, but Jesus Christ the son of God. The old and new Testaments was written by Jews, Jesus is the Messiah of the Jews and Saviour of all nations. In the gospel of Matthew; The Magi inquired;

> *"Where is He who has been born King of the Jews?"*
> *and Jeremiah; "Behold I will make a new covenant*
> *with the house of Israel and with the house of*
> *Judah." ....*

My entire missionary work was to make Israel conscious of this relationship, who can never be broken. We have made progress in science, art, literature, social life, only in religion is there any stagnation. ......People of brilliant intellectual powers have paid homage to Him, the Jew Spinoza declared; "Jesus is the highest symbol of Jewish wisdom." Jean Jacques Rousseau the French philosopher wrote; "If the death of Socrates was the death of a sage, then the death of Jesus was the death of a God." Strauss, who wrote several works to prone that Jesus is not God, declares that He is the highest goal to wish we can aspire in our thoughts. Ernest Renan, who caused a great many people to doubt the divinity of Jesus, finally says, that His beauty is eternal and that His kingdom will never come to an end. True belief in Jesus breaks down barriers, between races and nations."

With that Richard and Sabina stood up with King Michael, Daniel and Marguerite.

So David, Judith and their friends stood up also, together holding hands. Richard started to pray, inviting everyone to receive the gift of God "Jesus the Christ" as their Messiah. David, Judith and their friends, were move with emotion, and they all did it!

Chapter 17

A NEW LIFE

Judith jubilant; "David my parents are so conservative, and from generation to generation, they have practiced Judaism. I think we must keep quiet about our conversion, and let them notice the change in our lives."

"Good idea, it's not necessary to create more sorrow to them." replied David.

The next day all their friends accompanied them to the Orly airport, holding on to each other, dancing and singing a Jewish song that said; "Let us go back to Jerusalem"

David and Judith's parents were waiting with their son Slhomo with anticipation for their arrival. They could not believe their eyes, when they saw David and Judith with big smiles on their faces.

David hugged his mother and Shlomo, then Lydia, and said to her; "Lydia! That was the best experience of our lives, Thank you!"

Lydia responded; "Don't thank me, that was Elisabeth Blomberg's idea!"

Judith put her arms around her mother's shoulder and said;"Mother do you remember Madame Marguerite? she is married to Daniel, who is the cousin of King Michael of Romania, we had a marvellous time together. I have so much to tell you."

Chapter 18

YIGAEL YADIN

David back to work, was thrilled to meet with Yigael Yadin, Israel's most celebrated hero and Biblical archaeologist. Yigael was fifteen when he joined Haganah, the underground defence force of a jewish community in Palestine. There he required the name "Yadin" secret code name, it means, "will judge". Yigael Yadin became Haganah's chief of operations in 1947-1948 and chief of staff during Israel's war of independence. David was captivated by Yadin's personality and especially, by the story he told him about, when Yadin and his team explored caves in the area where the original Dead Sea Scrolls were found. There he found packets of letters. Only after the crumbly ancient papyrus was expertly unrolled, could the letters be read. Some of which had been written or dictated by Bar Kochba (also call Bar-Kokhba) the hero of the second Jewish revolt against Rome (132 AD-135 AD). Yadin and his teams were invited to the home of the president of Israel Yitzchak Ben Zvi, to report on their discoveries. Also was present the prime minister David Ben Gurion, and members of the Cabinet and of the Knesset. Yadin turned to the president of Israel and said; "Your excellency, I am honoured to be able to tell you that we have discovered fifteen dispatches written or dictated by the last president of ancient Israel 1800 years ago Bar Kochba! " Yadin explained, for a moment the audience seemed to be struck dumb. Then the silence was shattered with spontaneous cries of astonishment of joy.

Yadin and David became immediately friends.

Sunday evening Yadin stopped at David home. Judith invited Yadin to stay for dinner, and said; "Please Yadin tell me your side of the story about the war against Egypt in 1948, everyone called a miracle"

Yadin exclaimed; "Yes it was! Our God is always the same if we seek Him with all our heart He will answer! The book of Daniel says;

> *"But the people who know their God shall prove themselves strong, and shall STAND FIRM and take action for God."*

When we discovered that the Egyptian army was marching to take over Palestine, Every living soul was ready to fight. We did not have artillery, almost no munitions, very few weapons, we used what ever we had for weapons. The British were giving artillery, tanks and arms to the Egyptians. American authority refused to let American Jews to come help us. They forbid permits for them to fly to Israel to bring military weapons so we could defend ourselves. America had a pact with the Arabs for their oil. The British controlled Palestine from 1940 to 1948.

An American Jewish pilot Al Schwimmer a TWA flight engineer, became the master mind of the operation to find planes, ammunitions, weapons and pilots willing to lose their citizenships and face imprisonement and became outlaws to try to save Israel. Al Schwimmer became the FBI's most wanted for clandestine work at mobilising Jewish pilots living in America. …...The hotel 14 in New York was the meeting place of Haganah's US chief Yehuda Arazi. He found some German Nazi's planes captured under WW2 for sale in Panama and weapons in Czechoslovakia. He bought two B 17 and two other Bombers and a total of nine planes. …........Lou Levart fighter pilot, was flying to Tel Aviv with German weapons and munitions then fly back to Czechoslovakia to help the other pilots fix the planes they had purchased. Lou developed a strategy to attack the Arab army. He said to the others pilots; "We cannot wait any longer 10.000 Egyptian tanks will attack Tel Aviv tomorrow." …........They answer him, but those planes are not ready! Lou told them; "Ready or not, we must go and fly to save Israel." They came in those Nazi planes. How ironic is that? to save us! They destroyed the Egyptian army tanks by surprise, when there was no hope for us to survive. They came like an army of angels."

Judith and David were so taken by the story, they sat silent with their mouth open.

Yadin continued; "If one day you go to visit Czechoslovakia, there is a monument with the inscription: "IN COMMEMORATION OF THE PILOTS OF HAGANAH SQUADRON WHO TRAINED HERO FOR THEIR STRUGGLE FOR AN INDEPENDENT STATE OF ISRAEL IN THE YEAR 1948."

Yigael Yadin, took out his wallet and showed them a photo of the pilots: Shelly "Ike" Eichel, Marty Ribakoff, Bill Novick, Edward "Eddie" Styrak, who was not a Jew, Sam Lewis, Reynol "Roy" Selk, Sam Willi Sosnow, Eddie Harold, Lou Levart

Chapter 19

WHAT DOES IT MEAN, TO BE A MUSLIM?

Not long after David and Judith became Messianic believer they became friends with doctor Irmao Yousef, a Moroccan of a noble Muslim family, who was a brilliant speaker and articulate spokesman.

After dinner with Yadin and doctor Yousef David asked doctor Irmao; "What does it means to be a Muslim?"

"Thank you for asking me to explain this to you", responded doctor Yousef; "All Muslims believe that the Bible was falsified by the Jews. In their view, the true God-written Bible was taken into heaven with Jesus when the people wanted to crucify Him, That's why Jesus didn't die on the cross. As a result, He didn't pay the high price for us, and there was no salvation from our sins. I shared this conviction during my life in Morocco. What's the first thing that comes to mind when you hear the word Muslim "terrorist, suicide bomber, polygamist," Remember, our struggle is not against Muslims, Buddhists, Catholics, but against Satan and his angels. I love the Muslim people, I was once one of them and my family still belongs to them. But I'm against the radical theology that they preach. Islam is based on five pillars.

The first pillar is called "SHAHADA" Anyone who wants to adopt Islam as their religion is obliged to take this first step: they must go to a mosque, see a religious leader, and speak with him. Then, when everyone is present he raises his index finger in the middle of the crowd, goes forward, and loudly repeats the words of the leader in Arabic, which is considered to be the language of God: "I believe that there is no god but Allah; I believe that Mohammed is the last prophet." And all the people say;

Allahu Akbar, Allahu Akbar! Which means, "God is most great!"

The second pillar is "SALAT," which means "prayer." Muslims pray toward Mecca five times a day. When they pray, it is not speaking to God as we do. They do not consider Him a trusted friend or loving father. His prayer consists of rituals and memorised passages of the Koran. Muslim must wash his hand, feet, eyes, and ears, before praying, because Allah doesn't speak to impure and dirty people.

The third pillar is "ZAKAT," which means "alms." it literally means, "that which purifies my income." Not our leftovers. That is very important 2.5% of all funds and goods, this is for needy Muslim.

The fourth pillar is "SIYAM" and means "fasting" This represents Ramadan, a meaningful month, not only in terms of giving up food for 30 days, but it is a symbol of faith and religion. And it's during the month of Ramadan that God forgives the sins of the Muslims.

The last pillar is "HAJJ" which means "pilgrimage," Mohammed the prophet returned to his city, Mecca a few years after he had been expelled. Every Muslim has a duty to travel there at least once in his lifetime.

I've traveled to Mecca several times with my father, I'll never forget what happened there. A year before I moved to Paris to study. We were walking around Al-Kaaba, when I suddenly felt my father's strong hand holding me and pressing me against the wall of the building. He covered me with a white veil and pled, "Oh God! Show mercy on my son and all his descendants. Guard my son wherever he goes."

Four years later, I gave my life to Jesus Christ. I firmly believe that was the true God that answered my father's prayer on that day.

I remember my first day of university, when I saw all the different people. Nobody cared whether someone was black, white, Muslim, Atheist, Christian, Jew, Arab or European. I was just one of many, but deep in my heart I was convinced that I was better than everyone else there, because they were all nothing but filthy sinners in my eyes. I have always had exaggerated habits, don't forget that I had grown up in a rich and powerful family. The plane you're flying on belongs to the royal family. And on the weekends, I returned to Morocco no matter how high the cost. I'm ashamed to have once led such a self-indulgent and wasteful lifestyle. Since Christ redeemed me, I wouldn't trade my life now for all the riches in the whole world. Today I can say that I belong to the real royal family. I'm a child of the King of Kings, and the most precious blood, the blood that was shed on Calvary has cleansed me. There isn't enough money in the world to pay the high price that Jesus Christ paid for me. No body can obtain eternal life with money. I remember an experience that a friend once had. He was a company representative, working in Dubai. While he was presenting his project, he found that all the Muslims present left the room the moment they heard the call to prayer from the mosque. They didn't want to miss the time of prayer at any cost.

He told me with great awe of how God had spoken to his heart that day and said;

"How are you going to tell these people who pray five times a day about Jesus, if you don't have a prayer life yourself?"

Yadin and David, kept silent for a short time, then David said; "That makes me think that for sure I need to pray more, thinking about God and honor Him, instead to worry and be all wrapped up in all the circumstances we are facing today, because God is the only one who can do something about it, and guide us."

Yadin said;" Yes! that was also, the only way I was able to discover evidence to confirm Josephus' descriptions, the history of Masada, Bar Kochba and Herod's ceremonial palace also the biggest collection of Jewish and Roman coins of the first century A.D were found in one excavation!"

A strong knocking on the door, interrupted their conversation. The soldier at the door announced that David and Yadin were ordered to report immediately to headquarters.

Chapter 20

ASTONISHED

As director of intelligence for the northern border of Israel, David learned from agents behind the Syrian lines, that the Syrians were amassing tanks and men to attack Israel. The Golan Heights were crucial for defending Israel from the coming multi-nation Arab attacks.

David went to report to Uzi Narkiss, the general commanding Central Command, and said to him; "The Syrians have enormous equipped army, ready to come over the Golan Heights against us tomorrow. We have less than one full division of soldiers. Without divine intervention, we are doomed!"

The Chief Rabbi of the Israel Defence Forces. General Shlomo Goren, told David;"Your men are making history. What is going on in Sinai is nothing compared to this."

General Narkiss told Goren to Prepare his shofar, (trumpet) the traditional ram's horn – to mark the victory.

David learned that Shlomo Goren, came from Poland with his parents in 1925, when he was eight years old. At 12 he was recognised as a religious prodigy, and published his first work of rabbinical commentary when he was 17 years old. In 1948, he fought in the War of Independence, in which he was noted for his bravery, and was appointed chief chaplain of the Israel Defence Forces.

General David Weis cautiously led his men up the slope to the Golan Heights plateau, expecting to be assailed at any moment. The closer they came to where they were, surely the enemy must be.... David kept feeling that they were walking into a trap, but kept advancing with his men towards the plateau. Suddenly, an unexpected strong wind storm came upon them. David ordered his men to stop and cover themselves.

Fifteen minutes later, as the wind subsided, they beheld and astonishing sight. The wind had uncovered a minefield that would have surely ended them all had they kept advancing. As the men diffused the mines, all were keenly aware of the miracle that they had received from God. A strong feeling of peace came upon David.

Chapter 21

THE BATTLE FOR JERUSALEM

On May 25th, 1967, state-controlled Cairo Radio had announced, "The Arab people are firmly resolved to wipe Israel off the map." encouraged by President Nasser, four Arab States, Syria, Iraq, Jordan and Saudi Arabia – moved troops to Israel's borders.

As she had been in 1948, so also in 1967, Israel was outnumbered and outgunned. A total of 264,000 Israeli troops, most of them conscripted civilians. Confronted five Arab states with at least as many regular soldier. Israel's 800 tanks faced 2,504 Arab tanks. Israel's 300 combat aircraft were outnumbered by 680 Arab fighter and bomber aircraft. At its narrowest point, Israel's 50 kilometre (30 miles) central axis was a mere 14 kilometres (9miles) from the sea. Tel Aviv's beaches were only 25 kilometres (15 miles) from the nearest Arab border. The Israeli Minister of Defence, Moshe Dayan, warned the Government that the one chance of avoiding defeat was to strike first.

David and his men took control of the Golan Heights. The Jordanians, were driven 50 kilometres (30miles) eastward, out of West Bank and East Jerusalem, to the Jordan River. The cost of the war was high for those who had wished to destroy Israel. More than 15,000 Egyptian soldiers, several thousand Jordanian soldiers and 1,000 Syrian soldiers were killed. Israel's losses were 766 on all three fronts. All the Israelis recognised the Hand of God and gave Him all the Glory.

For the first time in its history Israel faced the problems of an occupying power, responsible for the lives and livelihoods of more than a million Palestinian Arabs in the West Bank and Gaza Strip. Under the Jordanian and Egyptian rule, these refugees had been neglected, and been maintained in their camps by the resources of the United Nations, and not integrated into the wider Arab society.

David hurried back to his parents farm 30 miles out of Jerusalem, where Judith, Shlomo and their friends took refuge during the six days of war. David was so relieved to see everyone safe and both his parent's home and Judith parent's were intact. Judith ran into David's arms screaming; "It was supernatural, like an army of angels all around this place to protect us!"

Everybody was anxious to hear David's story of the battle...... What a glorious day to be able to be together to celebrate another miraculous victory of Israel.

Jacques, Judith's father, opened the Bible and read; *"For he who touches you, touches the apple of My eye."* says the Lord (Zechariah chapter 2).

Chapter 22

THE LAZARUS FOUNDATION

Elisabeth Blomberg was very pleased that the whole family from both sides insisted she stay with them as long as she wanted. After all, she was now part of the family. They also hosted many friends from the town, since the war started, it was like a small Kibbutz. The farm was very spacious and everyone worked doing different chores.

Elisabeth was concerned about her friend Joseph. She said to Judith; " I think it will be a good time for us to go visit my friend. Shlomo will probably like to visit him."

Judith was curious, "Your friend Joseph? Hum... The single man, yes lets go."

They drove on the road to Ramallah. There on 30 acres all gated land, was a sign that read, "THE LAZARUS FOUNDATION"

Shlomo couldn't believe his eyes, in the middle of nowhere was something that looked like paradise. Elisabeth introduced Judith and Shlomo to Joseph who was in his 50's, middle stature, blue eyes, with a big smile.

He hugged Elisabeth, and said; "I was worried about you being in Jerusalem in the center of the war, but I know your faith in God. Although I wished you would be here, the foundation is a very safe place."

Elisabeth and Judith, gave the late good news, about the miraculous victory. During that time, Shlomo was interacting with cats, dogs and birds.

Shlomo asks Joseph; "Were did all those animals come from? Did you buy them?"

Joseph responds; "They were all rescued, they are my friends."

Judith observed Shlomo who was now 12 years old. It was the first time she saw him full of joy since his brother Zeke had died. He had birds on his head, and a cat in his arms.

Shlomo said; "Oh mother I want to live right here, this place is so lovely."

Shlomo thought he was in heaven. After about a hour he knew he was going to become a veterinarian, and he would come to work with Joseph.

Judith exclaimed; "what about your career as a concert pianist?"

He answered; "I can do both, because I love music and I love animals."

They all were laughing. Joseph took him for a tour to explain to him how to care for the animals.

Elisabeth and Judith walked around exploring. Judith asks; "How did you meet Joseph?"

She responds; "I met his parents years ago. They were both doctors. They did not have any children. They traveled a lot in many countries. When they visited Poland, they were appalled to see the exploitation of orphans in communist orphanages. They were like prison labor camps. During their visit to one orphanage, they donated two months of their time to heal some of the children, bringing medicine and performing surgery. They noticed a 6 year old boy, not talking not smiling not crying, sitting alone in a corner, with very sad eyes. They asked the woman in charge, about him. She told them, he is a sick boy, he never talks and will probably never express any feelings as he avoids being with people and children. He is not deaf because he respond to noise or voice, putting his hands on his ears. Intrigued they decided to adopt him and give him the name Joseph. .....Joseph's parents were in a concentration camp where Joseph was born. His parents died there. Joseph was mistreated until a prisoner friend of his mother escaped and took him with him. Then he dropped him at this orphanage. That was the only story they knew about his past, no name, no birth certificate. His adopted parents noticed that animals were attracted to him. God created animals for a good reason, they feel the hurt in people and their emotions, they have a special sense. Dogs, cats and horses became Joseph's best therapists. He learn to talk, laugh and cry with them. The animals healed his soul. Now Joseph heals animals, he understands them."

Judith and Elisabeth waited for Shlomo and Joseph to come back from the tour.

Shlomo was fascinated watching Joseph handle ferocious lions and tigers, Joseph would sit and lie down next to them, rubbing their backs and stomachs. Back from the tour, Shlomo jumped from the Jeep running to Judith, screaming; "Mother! Mother! You should see what Mister Joseph did! it was amazing ! And look, you see this grey pit bull, he adopted me, he chose me! He is mine, please mother, can we take him home? Grand-parents told me I can bring anything I want to the farm."

Judith answer him; "First let me call your dad, he will decide about that."

Judith called David and explained what happened. David laughed and said; "I always wanted a dog when I was young and never got one, I guess now is the right time, a dog will be a good friend for Shlomo."

Judith looked at Shlomo who was holding his breath. She said to him; "Dad said yes!"

Shlomo was jumping and dancing with joy screaming; "Yes!" He was holding the grey pit bull's head looking him in the eyes and said; "Your name is "Blue."

Joseph put a nice collar and a leash on "Blue". Shlomo could hardly hold the 4 year old happy dog.

David was overjoyed with the new addition to the family. Blue's, special place was near Shlomo's bed. And became his faithful companion.

Chapter 23

STOP!
LOOK!
LISTEN!

Chaim Weis, David's father who was a scientist and an atheist all his life, had a change of heart after his grandson, Zeke, had died all because of Elisabeth. Elisabeth was also a scientist, she came in their life with her own tragic testimony. It was not only what she said, but the way she was acting, that he saw God was real in her. He stopped to argue about; "God is the opium of the poor simple minded people"

Chaim and Sarai his wife loved Elisabeth as their own daughter. She was the spiritual strength of the family. David called her "My Rabbi!" Since Elisabeth moved with her adopted family, she enjoyed the fresh air at the farm, especially to be living with her best friend Judith. Her love and wisdom was priceless to everyone. Every morning at four o'clock she started to pray for each of them. Elisabeth's room was near Judith and David's room, their job on the front line was continually endangered by terrorist attack's.

This particular morning Elisabeth felt in her spirit the urgency to pray with them before they went to work.

The clock rang at 4:30 am. David hurried into the shower to get ready for work. The window was wide open to the garden and the fragrance of a multitude of flowers put a smile on Judith's face before she joined David in the shower.

A cup of tea in their hands, they both started to revise their files before going to their Headquarters near Jerusalem. A knock on the bedroom door disturbed them from their work.

Judith opened the door. Surprised to see Elisabeth, she asked her; "Are you OK?"

In an urgent tone of voice she responded; "We need to talk!"

Judith whispering; "Elisabeth please not now, we need to review our files for our superiors."

Elisabeth, forced herself into the room, and put her arm on Judith shoulder.

Elisabeth continued; "It is very important to put God first, before anything, if you want His protection!"

David interrupted her; "What? Elisabeth you don't understand we must get ready!"

The sun slowly started to rise entering the room.

Elisabeth almost shouted; "Stop! Look! Listen!"

David and Judith startled by the tone of authority in her voice. They stopped what they were doing, a questioning look on their face.

Elisabeth continued; "Your day not only involves yourself, but the lives of many people. It is imperative that you seek God first. Jesus said; "If you love Me you will obey Me and put all your burden at my feet." We have a powerful God who loves us and He has something to say to you right now!"

Elisabeth fell on her knees, followed by David and Judith. The sunrise shinning on Elisabeth's face. Touched with emotion Elisabeth said; "Yes Lord I listen…"

They received a message from the Lord trough the mouth of Elisabeth;

"IF YOU STAY FAITHFUL IF YOU HOLD MY HAND I WILL LET YOU SEE MY KINGDOM YOUR PLACE WILL BE NEAR ME I ALREADY PREPARED YOUR PLACE. FEAR NOT THE WORLD AND DON'T LOOK AT THEIR DEEDS BECAUSE YOU MUST LIVE IN THE WORLD BUT YOU ARE NOT LIKE THEM. WHEN TRIBULATION WILL FALL AROUND YOU, YOU WILL NOT FEAR BECAUSE MY HAND WILL KEEP YOU FAR FROM THE CALAMITY. HOLD ONTO MY HAND KEEP YOUR EYES ON ME!"

David was convicted and he said; "Yes Lord I will stop look and listen to your voice!"

The peace of God's presence filled the room.

THE END